Learnings from Little Ones

"Tales from a grandfather's heart"

by
Gilman Smith

First Edition

— be a child

Gil Smith

Papaco Press   *Frisco, Colorado*

Published by

Papaco Press
P.O. Box 2714
Frisco, Colorado 80443

Second Printing
Printed in the United States of America
ISBN: 0-9669875-0-0 $12.95 Soft cover

acknowledgments

editing
Jeff Brandberg
Jack Salter
Billie Stanton

cover artwork
published from an
original pencil drawing
"Let's Go Grandpa!"
by J. D. Hillberry

consulting
Bob Moscatelli, author
<u>Too Soon Old, Too Late Smart</u>

layout
Laura Norman

❤

dedication

To my wife Susan, that cute little blond girl I met when I was 8 years old.

To my children: Kim, Stephanie and David who have taught me much more than I taught them.

To my grandchildren: Zach, Nicholas, Connor, Jake, Parker, Kari, River and Dylan who have resurrected my feelings of "awe" and "ahhh", and given me lots of hugs.

To all "Little Ones" everywhere.

♥

About the Author

Gil Smith was born in New England, but grew up in a small town in western Pennsylvania. His family moved there when he was 8. The day the moving van arrived, an 8-year-old, blond-haired little girl rode down the street on her bicycle to look the new kid over. Fifty two years later Susan and Gil are still riding bikes, holding hands and celebrating life. The closeness of their families in their close-knit neighborhood have had a profound effect on them.

After an extensive career in the steel-making business, that moved him all across the United States and Canada, Gil retired to the mountains of Colorado. Today, he teaches skiing to preschoolers at Breckenridge Ski Resort, reads to kids at Zoomers Preschool and serves on the Children's Ministry Committee at his church. In addition, he sends rocks, leaves, animal bones and an occasional dead snake to his grandchildren in Denver and Atlanta.

Table of Contents

Preface

This book began the day my first grandchild, Zachary Gilman Schorr was born. Until then, I could only imagine what being a grandfather was like. But, when I held him in my arms for the very first time, my heart, my soul, my life was changed forever. I was speechless and began to cry. Emotions I could never have imagined now effervesced through my entire body like bubbles from a freshly opened bottle of champagne. Now I knew. Now I could feel the feeling. Now my heart soared. Now my heart tingled. Now I was a grandfather!

Since Zach's birth, the miracle has continued. The birth of each of my other grandchildren: Nicholas, Connor, Jake, Parker, Kari, River and Dylan have intensified my feelings to a level that almost scares me. I write them letters, poems, prayers and epistles. I send them postcards from airports, and trinkets from far away places. My heart jumps each time the phone rings in anticipation of the "Hi Papa!" at the other end. They are literally always on my mind.

The writings that follow are "learnings" or lessons I have learned from children, mostly under 6 years old. There are three exceptions: The essay entitled "Dr. Demming" is about a 90-year-old professor, a profound thinker, with the simplicity of a child. "The Teacher" is about my son David who, at age 21, taught me to "let go". The letter to Zachary entitled "Raton Road" is from the "awe" in me. I never could have written it before I became a grandfather.

❤

Learnings

"Learnings" are discoveries. Learnings happen when a light goes on in your head, and you say to yourself, "ahhh!" or "ah-hah!" Learnings also happen when you experience "awe." Awe is an emotion of wonder caused by some thing or some event: like a snow-capped mountain on a blue-sky-day; like a red-orange sunset over a glassy sea; like your daughter gliding down the stairs in her wedding gown; like a baby drawing its first breath, then bellowing to announce her arrival. Awes are a lot like "wows".

These writings, or "learnings", came about when I experienced an "ahhh" or an "awe" or a "wow", especially when I was with Zach, Nicholas, Connor, Jake, Parker, Kari, River and Dylan.

Today, I am much more aware of the "learnings" in my life. When I'm with little ones, I am swept away by their spontaneity, their innocence and their simple perspective of things. Their untainted minds comprehend life and life's happenings with a stark reality and understanding, without all the façades of adults.

I hope these stories help you rediscover a part of yourself.

I hope they help you increase your awareness of the "learnings" that surround you every day.

I hope you find lots of "awes" and "ahhhs".

❤

Born to be a Grandpa

I was born to be a grandfather. My friend Charlie Salanski, who preceded me in grandfatherhood by about 8 years, once told me, "being a grandfather is one of the very few things in life that is absolutely everything it's cracked up to be." He was right! Something magical about it defies description. I don't know if it's the dramatic increase in hugs, the "specialness" of this child-of-a-child sitting on your lap, or the receiving of such an unconditional gift of unconditional love. It doesn't matter, it's indescribable and it's wonderful.

The pencil drawing on the cover of this book pretty well sums it up: the time-worn hand of a grandfather whose little finger is being tugged on by a tiny, fresh, uncalloused hand eager to go for a walk. It is a wonderful feeling to have a "little one" invite you along for some new adventure, holding on for security, yet firmly leading the way. My daughter gave it to me for Christmas when Jake was almost 2.

Jake and I take lots of walks. Once, it took us an hour to walk around the block, stopping to look at ants, drawing pictures in the dirt and literally stopping and smelling the roses in Mrs. Dwyer's yard.

Yes, I was born to be a grandpa. It's my job, and I love it. Maybe, for the first time in my life, I have a mission: "To relate to little ones in such a way as to give them a positive feeling about themselves; to listen to them, no matter how long it takes; to help them learn about the ways of nature; to let them lead when taking walks; and to learn from their wisdom."

These days, folks are awfully busy with their lives. There doesn't seem to be enough hours in the day. Well, I've got a solution to this problem. It will relieve stress, lower blood pressure, simplify life, and be of benefit to another person: Simply set aside one hour, just for today, to spend with a "little one." You don't have to plan anything, just listen and follow the instructions. If you get bored, stick with it and become more involved. If you don't try to run the show, I think you'll find yourself smiling a lot and acting like a kid again. What fun! What a good feeling! What a blessing, for you and your little one! Kids need to know an "older person" they can have fun with and relate to. They need to know someone who loves them just as they are, not for what they will become.

So, when the time comes, let yourself go. Get down on the floor and discover the world of little kids. Take off your watch and forget about time. Read them books. Go for meaningless walks. Give them lots of hugs. It's the greatest high you'll ever experience, and it doesn't cost a dime - until grandma goes shopping.

Bon Voyage!

♥

Bonding

I have a picture on my dresser of Zach and me sitting on one of those white metal backyard chairs gazing off into space. He is 9 months old and I am, well, I'm the grandpa. Before he could walk, Zach would sit on my lap, nestled into the crook of my arm, and we would observe. For maybe an hour or so we would just sit in that chair and rock and look at things. Neither of us would make a sound, we'd just observe. We observed the sky. We observed the clouds. We observed an old man shuffling down the street. We observed grass, trees, flowers, birds and butterflies and bugs. We listened to the backyard sounds of summer: squirrels squawking at Alex, Zach's golden retriever, mocking birds warbling, crickets chirping and, in the distance, kids riding their bikes and laughing at the sun.

It was one of the most peaceful, serene times I've ever experienced. No speaking, no looks, just this little kid sitting on his grandpa's lap sharing the happenings of the day.

I've made a special point of spending some "observing time" with each of my grandkids. Somehow there is an understanding that mysteriously joins our spirits. Somehow the two of us are brought together by this sharing. I can't really explain it, but I know it is very real - a magical communion between two of God's children at different places on their journeys.

I don't think the kids will remember our "sitting" time, at least not in the memory banks of their minds, but I believe there is a memory bank in the heart. Perhaps the feeling of my arm curled securely around them, and the calm serenity of awe that we both experienced will be stored in there. It's definitely stored in mine.

Thanks Zach.

❤

Flowers, Bugs and Pine Cones

Alexandrea, I called her Alex for short, was about 3 when she came to visit us with her parents. It was August, and the Colorado summer days were absolutely perfect with 75° highs and 50° lows. Alex was beautiful, an only child of 30-something parents. She had learned early on that she was the princess of the household. She was a joyful bundle of energy.

Her long, blond ringlets bounced up and down as we trekked to Lily Pad Lake. The trail wound through aspen groves and lodgepole pine, like a meandering stream. There were flowers to smell, rocks to throw, pine cones to examine and an occasional chipmunk or squirrel to chase. I chuckled at her exuberance, as her sparkling face scampered from discovery to discovery.

The snowpack had been deep the past winter, and the resultant puddles and wetlands had produced a bumper crop of bugs - especially mosquitoes.

Nothing like back East, mind you, but still enough to be irritating. My little princess-hiking mate had the sweet smell of freshly shampooed hair, which attracted every insect within 100 yards. I smeared some repellent on our arms and necks, and we took off down the trail examining rocks and picking up twigs.

We reached Lily Pad Lake in about an hour and checked out the huge beaver hut on the south shore. The beavers were napping, I guess. After about 20 minutes of exploring, we decided to head home. We retraced our steps around the lake and started up the trail. Suddenly, Alex plopped herself down on a log and began complaining and whimpering. She was tired and the novelty of the excursion had worn off. I tried to coax her forward, but she whined and pleaded with me to carry her. I picked her up and stumbled up the dirt path. Five minutes was about my limit, so I put her down despite her efforts to cling to my neck. She cried, and I tried to reason with her, to no avail. In desperation, I pointed to some blue columbine flowers about 20 feet down the trail. She ventured over and touched them gently, pulling them to her cute little turned-up nose and inhaling the fragrance. About 30 paces farther she spotted a daddy-long-legs skittering over some stones; farther on, a pine cone, then more flowers. I picked her up and gave her a hug. She gave me a smile.

Slowly but surely, we progressed: flower by flower, bug by bug, pine cone by pine cone, rock by rock; animal tracks, birds, fallen logs and tiny pebbles. We reached the car in about an hour and a half.

What a great hike! How tedious and impossible some journeys seem when we first look at them. Yet how enjoyable they can be when we take them one step, one flower at a time. A cliché perhaps, but true. We adults are continually bombarded with sage advice to plan ahead, look at the big picture, save for retirement, etc. I agree with all these things, but life actually happens one minute at a time, and in that minute we can hug each other, smell the roses, smile, skip a stone, meditate, pray and examine a pine cone - even when we're weary.

The long term is simply a bunch of moments, and living in each present moment is the joy of life.

Thanks Alex.

❤

Back to the Future

They called it "early retirement," but it was really the ax. The company I had worked for, for 29 years was downsizing and merging, so I was one of the ones to go. For someone of my generation who thought of working for one company until age 65, this was a real ego blow. Nowadays, people change jobs every 5 years or so, and getting axed can actually be a plus on your resumé, but that's another story. Anyway, I retired early and promptly set about wondering what I was going to do with the rest of my life. Do I have enough money? Will I be able to get another job? Should I get another job? I laid awake at night ruminating over why I had been forced out.

My wife suggested we get out of town for a while, so we headed to Atlanta to visit our daughter and spend time with our first grandson, Zachary. After all, I now had all the time to do those things I wanted to do when I didn't have time to do them. Besides, Zach had grown from a scrawny, blotchy-faced newborn into a grinning 1-year-old bundle of energy and joy, and some "joy" was just what I needed.

One morning, I offered to baby-sit while my wife and daughter ran some errands and went to the grocery store. After 4 or 5 stories, several trips up and down the stairs, a drink of milk and some animal crackers, I was exhausted and ready for a nap. Zach, however, wanted to go outside, so I followed him as he toddled toward the front door in that wobbly way little kids move forward, with their tiny feet hurrying to catch up with their teetering body. Wouldn't it be wonderful, I thought, if we were all so eager to go somewhere, anywhere, just to feel this wild propulsion of our semi-controlled bodies hurtling forward? Zach propelled himself toward the big wooden door gurgling and babbling all the way. He pounded on the door with the slap, slap, slap of his half-pint hand and squealed with delight as I swung it in its wide arc, revealing another beautiful summer day.

Dew was on the grass, and the flowers in the bed to the right of the steps looked as if they had just awakened. They seemed to smile as the morning sun warmed their petals. Zach and I stood, looking out, me staring blankly at the street before us, and Zach wide-eyed at all the world before him; me with feelings of corporate rejection, and Zach with feelings of awe and pure joy; me with feelings of hurt and anxiety, and Zach with feelings of bliss and excitement, his toothless grin immersed in the early morning light. My stomach growled, refocusing my attention on that cold knot in my gut. Zach turned and pitter-patted back toward the family room.

I found a new job in about 6 months. It was even better than the one I had "retired" from. All those sleepless nights, all that spinning in my brain, all that resentment and self-pity for nothing!

Oh, to be more childlike!
Oh, to be so excited about today!

Oh, to know no fear!
Oh, for the eagerness of adventure!
Oh, to have awe!

Zach teaches. Papa learns.

❤

Hugs

Emily lives in England, somewhere near London, I think. She came to Colorado on a holiday with her parents, and after a long flight from Gatwick to Denver, they rented a car and drove to Breckenridge arriving in the early evening. They settled into their rented condo, ate a delivered cheese and pepperoni pizza and went to bed, trying desperately to adjust to the six-hour time change.

The following day, promptly at 9 a.m., Emily and her parents arrived at the Children's Ski School. Eager to experience the Colorado snow, they quickly signed all the forms and deposited 4-year-old Emily in the large room where 40 kids or so were playing before going outside to begin their lessons.

Emily was very shy and as she nervously surveyed her situation from under her light brown bangs, she began to cry softly. She missed her mommy already. No one noticed at first, but soon a few instructors spotted her tucked into a corner of the room. They tried to calm her. Some tried reading a book. Some showed her toys and a baby doll. Some introduced her to more outgoing kids, and some tried giving her a cookie or a glass of water. Nothing seemed to work.

When I noticed Emily, one of the well-meaning instructors was trying to reason with her. I knew from experience that rationalization wouldn't work, so I walked over, reached down and picked her up and hugged her without saying a word. She clung to me as we gently swayed back and forth. She felt so fragile to me, and, I imagine, I felt so strong to her. Finally, I felt her begin to relax and her weeping turned to sniffles. We kept swaying as I told her of the times I had been frightened and missed my mom. I asked her if she would draw me a picture and I lowered her to the floor as she nodded "yes." I've always been a hugger, but I learned something new from Emily that day.

There is a magical component to a meaningful hug: When an unconditional hug is given and that person responds in the same manner, a peaceful serenity evolves, if only for a minute. Perhaps it's because for an instant the two meld together and subconsciously realize that though they are both unique, they are not alone. What a wonderful feeling! What a special moment!

It's risky to hug: We might not be hugged in return. The other persons' personal space might be violated. The hug might be misinterpreted by the individual or observers. But, I believe its worth the risk. It's a gift from God.

Emily learned about skiing that day. I learned about hugs.

Thanks Em.

❤

Natures Way

Gentle waves washed the early morning beach as David and I strolled among the seaweed, shells and driftwood deposited by last night's tide. The morning chill was slowly being pushed aside by the warmth of the 9 o'clock sun. It looked like another beautiful summer day along the north Florida coast.

It was David's 3rd birthday, and he tip-toed down the shoreline, pausing to examine each new discovery: coconut husks and palm leaves from some tropical island, water-logged bits of wood and an occasional piece of rope from some passing ship. He stopped for a moment to probe a jellyfish partially submerged in the sand, then quickly resumed his journey.

"David!" I yelled, "Look! I think the jellyfish is still alive." I began to dig around its gelatin-like body. He turned and rushed back to examine the colorless blob. "Let's push him back in the water, maybe he'll live," I shouted above the whish of the incoming waves.

"No," he answered nonchalantly, "I think we should leave him alone. It's nature's way," and he scurried off down the beach.

I was stunned by my 3-year-old's matter-of-fact attitude, his frankness and simple comprehension of nature's laws. Somehow this little person, who had never experienced someone's or something's passing, understood that dying is a part of living. Why was my reaction to the struggling creature so different? Was it the rescuer in me - always wanting to make things right? Was it my grandiosity at work, writing headlines for the afternoon paper: Father and Son Save Jellyfish? Was it the fact that I had experienced more of life and that brought out the compassionate part of me?

I really don't know what was going on inside me; I only know I was amazed by David's remark.

Life is so simple to little kids. Adults make it so complicated.

"I think I'll just jog down the beach, catch up with David and see if I can learn more about nature's way."

Thanks David.

❤

Nicholas

Nicholas died on December 6th, less than 24 hours before he was born. He was my second grandson. The doctors said it had something to do with amniotic fluid.

He was a perfect little kid with a full head of beautiful black hair. He had perfect little features: ten perfectly formed little fingers, ten perfectly formed little toes, no deformities or anything - a perfect little kid.

The nurses urged me to spend a few private minutes with him, so they led me down the hall to a small, quiet room by the nursery. There they placed him gently in my arms. Feelings I had never experienced and still cannot adequately describe completely engulfed me.

As I held him, we bonded in some mysterious, mystical, spiritual way that transcends human experience and understanding. In the space of those few minutes, we took all the hikes in the woods, all the fishing trips, all the walks in the park, read all the bedtime stories and had all the giggles and laughs of a lifetime.

His body was limp in my arms, so I held him close to my tear-soaked chest. He was so beautiful, and I prayed to God that somehow this was just a nightmare. Somehow little Nicholas would suddenly start breathing, and I would jump up and shout the good news up and down the pastel halls of the maternity ward. I would go to the store and buy him a fishing pole, a baseball mitt and a toy truck. I would bounce him on my knee and smile as he laughed with glee. But it was not to be, and as the nurse took little Nicholas from my arms, I collapsed under the crush of the hurt and pain and helplessness. I felt cheated and I slumped to the floor, sobbing uncontrollably.

It's been almost 5 years now, and I'm beginning to heal. Looking back, I've learned a lot from Nicholas. I've learned that grief can be debilitating; grief can paralyze; grief can depress; grief can crush your heart and consume your mind. I've learned that I'm more vulnerable than I thought. I've learned to be a better listener and to empathize more with people in despair. I've learned to cry more and laugh more. I've learned to seek professional help when I need it. I've learned to feel deeper, to live with more zest, and to savor each moment of my existence.

Grief has many forms and many sources. Some, we work through very quickly. Others, like losing Nicholas, are heavy burdens and require a lot of hard work. I've come to believe that grief, of any kind, never goes away; it transforms. Like bread dough, grief needs time to grow, needs kneading, needs punching, needs rest, and then, more kneading, more punching, more rest. It needs heating up and cooling down to transform, and if we are patient and keep working on it; if we don't try to hurry things; if we don't ignore it or stuff it; if we keep struggling with it, a transformation will take place. The grief, which was once so crippling, will now sustain us, make us stronger, and enable us to experience the fullness and richness of each new day. It will become bread for our journey.

Nicholas gave me a gift. I'm stronger now, somehow, and life has more meaning. I still grieve losing him. I still ask why. I still have bouts of sadness. I still feel cheated, but I'm moving forward. I'm not crippled anymore. The experience of the past is enabling me to enjoy more todays, and I'm looking forward to more tomorrows. I'm beginning to be nourished by the bread.

Thanks Nicholas.

♥

Baseball

It was one of those wonderful bonding experiences, a Saturday morning trip to the hardware store with my grandson. The clerk smiled at this little kid with blond hair, bright blue eyes and a 3-year-old attitude. Connor bounced from aisle to aisle as we looked at the tools and plumbing supplies. No man can visit a hardware store without at least looking at the latest wrench or electric drill. I resisted buying any new gadgets, settling for a piece of plastic pipe to fix grandma's sink which, incidentally, was what we had come for in the first place.

The warm spring day stirred the little boy in me as we passed the city park. The ball field stood empty, devoid of any activity and stripped of everything including the bases, even home plate. I stopped the car in back of third base and we climbed the 6 stairs to the top of the old wooden bleachers. Most of the paint was long gone, worn off by years of cheers of mothers and fathers jumping up and down, encouraging their offspring and screaming at the "ump."

Connor and I talked about the Braves and home runs and fast pitches and the roar of the crowd. The field was empty and quiet. We climbed down the bleachers and started for the car when I noticed Connor was not with me. Turning around, I spotted him behind the backstop with his 3-year-old fingers clutching the partially rusted wires of the fence and his face pressed tightly against it. I beckoned him to come, but his mind was awash with images of heroes and home runs.

I walked to the pitcher's mound and announced in a loud voice, "Ladies and gentlemen, boys and girls, children of all ages, now batting for the Atlanta Braves, the best hitter in the whole world, Connor Schorr." He released his grip on the backstop and scampered to where home plate should be. "Tip your hat to your fans," I encouraged. He did. "Wave to your mother in the stands." A brief wave. He looked like a miniature

Babe Ruth as he pounded his imaginary bat on the imaginary home plate. He took 3 practice swings and readied the bat on his shoulders. I twisted the imaginary ball in my imaginary mitt. I glared at the batter and began my windup. The imaginary ball streaked toward the plate. Connor reared back and took a mighty swing. "Crack!" the bat sounded as the imaginary ball soared toward the center field fence. The announcer shouted, "There it goes ladies and gentlemen, a huge hit. Going! Going! Gone! It's a home run for the greatest hitter in the whole world."

Connor's little legs were pounding as his entire body strained to complete the circuit. He jumped on first base and headed for second. He rounded second and sped toward third. His face grimaced with effort and determination as he rounded third and headed for home. He crossed home plate proudly, still running hard and slowly came to a halt. The imaginary crowd was going wild! He swaggered to the bench, his hands on his hips, a smirk on his face.

"Tip your hat to the crowd," I hollered. He doffed his cap and twirled around. "Wave to your mother," and he waved.

It was almost 1 o'clock when his little legs gave out. There had been 23 pitches, 23 home runs, 23 roars of the crowd, and 23 swaggers to the bench. We sauntered to the car, and he crawled into the back seat. In 5 minutes he was fast asleep. It was the greatest game I had ever witnessed - no bat, no ball, no errors.

Thanks Connor.

♥

Mind Your Manners

Sally was a stunning bride in her long white gown, and nephew Jeff was very handsome in his black tuxedo. They had met after college and a whirlwind, long-distance romance followed. Finally, they decided to tie the knot.

Jeff loved to wrestle with my 3-year-old grandson Jake, so Jake was asked to be the ring bearer at the wedding. (Jake told everyone he was the "bear ringer.") He was all dressed up in his shiny, miniature black tux, with "racing stripes" on his black pants and a mirror shine on his black patent-leather shoes. He started down the aisle cautiously as the organ played. After 3 or 4 halting steps he whirled around and dashed back to his dad at the rear of the church. Again he started down the aisle only to bolt about halfway down and run back to the refuge of his father's arms. After two more aborted attempts, he finally made it to the altar and stood as tall as he could near "uncle Jeff." He was so proud, and Jeff smiled down at him.

I love weddings. They are such great family times. I get to dance with all the beautiful girls, joke with all the guys and generally exhibit all my eccentric personality traits, usually to the chagrin of my wonderful wife.

At the reception, we were all busy chitchatting with people we had not seen for awhile and people we were meeting for the first time. I was seated at one of those round banquet-hall type tables with, the quite attractive mother of one of the bridesmaids. She was on my left and "bear-ringer" Jake was on my right. Mother-of-a-bridesmaid and I were having a pleasant conversation as I munched on a sesame hard roll, washing it down with some delightful red wine. Suddenly, Jake tugged at my coat and blurted out, "Papa, don't talk with food in your mouth." I was mortified. Jake gave me one of those "gotcha papa" smiles and my wife roared with laughter. She had been admonishing me lately with those same words. Kids do say the darnedest things, and often at the darnedest times.

It was a good learning for me. Sometimes grandpas let ourselves go a little too much, not just in talking with our mouths full, but in lots of little ways, like not shaving for a couple of days, wearing our favorite golf shirt - even with old stains on it, neglecting to trim our ear and nose hairs and slurping our soup. If we want our grandkids to have good grooming habits, perhaps we need to pay a little more attention to ourselves. Like it or not, grandpas are role models.

I'll try to be better and not talk with my mouth full.

Thanks Jake.

♥

River

River was just a little kid, barely 3 months old. He was at that stage where an occasional smile would push away the blank stare of a new born trying to figure out what's going on. It's the time when a baby's personality begins to show. It's a wonderful time, full of hope and anticipation.

Each day, the change in little River was greeted with unbridled glee from his parents who usually called to tell us what new things he had done.

It's interesting how this little guy can communicate. If he cries, he either needs burped, fed, or his diaper changed. If he is tired, he simply falls asleep. If he is curious about something, he flails at it with his tiny little hands. If he is happy, he smiles - or maybe it's gas. In any case, River is a great communicator. He's so good at it, most times, he doesn't even have to do anything to get his needs met.

Sometimes I think my communication skills are so much more sophisticated than River's. I'm able to hem and haw, beat around the bush and try to, somehow, get inside the other person's head so that I can manipulate situations to get my own way. It takes a lot of time and I think I'm so persuasive.

Maybe if I spent more time and effort in being more direct about my needs, I'd get more of them fulfilled.

Thanks River.

❤

The Teacher

The room was dark except for some soft light in one corner. Peaceful music drifted through my consciousness as a voice softly droned. I was one of 30 businessmen who had enrolled in a seminar on leadership with the Atlanta Consulting Group. It was about 9 p.m. on the third day of our week-long session. Our minds had been challenged from early morning until late at night. We were all tired. Tonight we were being led through a visioning exercise to help us become more aware of the learning opportunities around us, even though we supposedly were skilled decision makers and were leaders extraordinaire.

The voice was leading our imaginations on a walk through a forest. The day was filled with sunshine and blue sky over-flowing into our spirit. The vegetation was lush and green with babbling brooks, hopping rabbits and scampering squirrels. Even the birds were celebrating the feeling. I walked along a well-trodden path winding its way through a golden aspen glen sprinkled with spruce and fir. Quietly, I emerged onto a hillside meadow blanketed with wild grass and dotted with wild flowers of every description. They called to me to lie down on the soft earth, but I resisted. The path before me wound up toward a solitary gnarled apple tree atop a knoll. There, next to the apple tree, stood a weather-beaten red schoolhouse - like the ones in Norman Rockwell paintings. As I meandered up the hill, I saw that the playground, once worn bare by games of baseball and ring-around-the-rosy was now overtaken by wild grass and weeds. The school bell that once summoned children to class hung rustily from the steeple. The door was ajar.

"Go on in," the soft voice commanded. the door creaked as I pushed it open. The wooden floor was dust covered but worn smooth from many days of little feet scurrying to their desks. Now, no desks were in the room. A small wooden chair stood centered in the front.

"Who's sitting in the chair?" the voice whispered, then paused. "This person is your teacher."

I was stunned and started to weep. I tried holding back, but the sobbing welled up inside me. My mind was exploding with the relevance of the moment, for there, sitting in the chair, was my 21-year-old son, David!

For the past 7 years, or so, David and I had had a tumultuous relationship. Me, trying to mold him into the stereotypical successful businessman; he, neglecting school and cutting classes. Me, pressuring him to focus on becoming a doctor, lawyer or corporate executive; he, spending time playing soccer and hangin' out. Every ounce of energy I could summon had been focused on making him something I thought he should be. What battles we had! Neither of us giving in, not even an inch.

Today, David is not a doctor, lawyer or corporate executive. Today, he's living his dream as a soccer coach with a lovely wife and two frisky sons. Today, we hug and laugh about our struggles. I tell him how he must be one helluva tough individual to have stood up to my rantings and ravings. Today, I ask him for his advice, and he asks me for mine. And today, tears still well up inside me when I recall that night I met him sitting in that chair, in the front of the room in the schoolhouse.

I'm still absorbing and discovering the meaning of that experience, but this I've learned: Trying to shape and mold another person is cheating them, and depriving them of their own self-discovery. How beautiful we all are when we discover our true selves!

I've also learned that teachers come in all sizes, shapes and colors. They are all around us everyday: in the forest and the meadow, in the schoolhouse, at the post office, next door, at work, at play, at church, everywhere, often right under our noses.   Learning comes from embracing them, wrestling with them and experiencing things with them - and learnings are the stuff of life.

Thanks David.

❤

Teeter-totter

The park was bathed in the 11 a.m. sun awaiting the onslaught of noonday joggers and playground kiddies. Jake and I had arrived about 10:30 and his 2-year-old legs had not stopped moving since. We had chased a dozen or so squirrels, 2 flocks of geese, and had shined the metal on the sliding board numerous times with the denim seat of his size 2 Levis. Life was good.

The clock inside my mind, which had ruled my life for so long as I hustled to business appointments and meetings, was now located in my heart. The face on the clock was still there, but the hands only appeared when I wanted them to: Like being home for dinner or going to the dentist. Today, there were no time pressures, and Jake and I simply wandered aimlessly, succumbing to whatever impulse came our way.

I hadn't noticed a teeter-totter for 30 years, but there one was, tucked away in an obscure part of the sandy playground. The red wooden seats I knew as a kid were made of red plastic now, but the worn steel pipe that separated them was still the same, teetering, more or less, on a rigid fulcrum. "C'mon Jake," I beckoned, "let's go on the teeter-totter!" We ran to the end resting on the ground, and as I lifted him onto the seat, he giggled with glee. I ran around to the end that was protruding into the sky and began to pull it down so I could get on. Jake's gleeful laughter abruptly stopped. His eyes widened in fright as my end went down and he levitated. His fright turned to tears, so I gently lowered him to the ground.

I was reminded of my boyhood chum Tommy Bowser. Tommy was a few years older than me, and one day we decided to teeter-totter at the local playground. We went up and down a few times and just as I began to relax and trust the cooperative teamwork of teeter-tottering, Tommy jumped off and I crashed to the ground, jarring every bone in my body. I cried and ran home, shattered that my friend had betrayed me. My relationship with Tommy was never quite the same after that.

I put my arms around Jake and tried to reassure him that I would take care of him. He was still frightened and wary. As I hugged him and talked softly in his ear, he gradually consented to being lifted off the ground. Little by little I increased the height until he was laughing and shouting with glee as we went up and down, up and down, up and down.

Oh the joy two people share when they trust each other unconditionally! To be able to trust a person is to receive a wonderful gift of serenity and peace from that individual. It's the most basic of ingredients in a relationship, and it's built on a history of actions, not just words.

Jake trusts me. I think I can handle the responsibility, but I don't take it lightly. I must constantly earn that trust again and again each time we are together. I must be careful with my promises, so I can keep them. No "little white lies". No last minute changes that betray his faith. No twisting of words to cover up.

I can't jump off unexpectedly. One slip, and trust is gone and just like Tommy Bowser and me, our relationship will never be the same. How fragile! How sacred! How joyful! How precious!

Thanks, Jake.

❤

Jealousy

The smile on her face lights up my heart. Her nose squiggles up and her blue eyes sparkle like a rainbow dancing over the lake. Kari is our first granddaughter and, as you can imagine, she's the princess of the family. She idolizes her older brother, Jake, and giggles and laughs at just about everything he does. Jake is 3 and a real bundle of boundless energy flitting around the house like the loose end of a garden hose. He ruled the roost until Kari came along, and now he's experiencing his first real taste of <u>really</u> sharing. For the first time he isn't getting all the attention. Oh, he's still the cool little kid who thinks he's a dinosaur monster. He still has just the right blend of mischievous and civilized behavior - in my opinion about an 80/20 mix, but his mother would like it the other way around. He's still very special, but now he must share his mom and dad's attention with his sister - and she's pretty demanding.

Jake's just a normal kid, experiencing

jealousy for the first time. There's no big problem here, in fact, it's kind of amusing to watch, but to Jake it's a bit of a problem having a little sister around. Frankly, I don't think he'd mind if she just disappeared. It makes me nervous when he grits his teeth and gives her one of those "brotherly" hugs. Sibling rivalry can be a serious issue if parents aren't aware of it, but if Kari survives all of Jake's "love," they'll grow to be best of friends, and Jake will protect her from all evil as only a big brother can.

I've learned a lot by watching this whole scenario develop and act out. I must confess, besides a chuckle, it gives me pause to examine some of my own relationships. How easy it is to become jealous or envious when someone else steals the show, grabs the spotlight, or has more, or does something better than me? Maybe it's a male thing, but I don't think so. I have to confess, I still get green with envy or jealous at times. Maybe it's an unhealthy piece of the competitive spirit I've fostered and espoused all my life? Maybe I'm not as secure as I think I am?

After all these years, I'm supposed to have my act together, but I know I don't, and I don't want anyone else to know. Maybe no one has their act together? Maybe not having my act together is just another part of being human? After all, older brothers show signs of it at the tender age of 3. It seems I'm always searching for perfection, when maybe just being human is the perfection I seek.

Thanks Jake.

Thanks Kari.

❤

Dr. Demming

Dr. Edwards Demming was the father of the modern-day Quality Movement in the United States. In the '50s and '60s, he attempted to convince General Motors, Ford and Chrysler to change their manufacturing methods to one of statistical process control, i.e. to control the various manufacturing steps so that each car that rolled off the assembly line would be free of defects. The companies would save millions of dollars because they wouldn't have to inspect their finished cars, and more important, they would eliminate the reworking process of correcting defects in finished products. GM, Ford and Chrysler ignored him.

The Japanese got wind of his theories and invited him to help in their automobile manufacturing plants. The rest is history: Japanese automobiles became the finest in the world and captured a huge market share in the U.S. Dr. Demming became the only non-Japanese person to ever receive the

Japanese Award of Merit.

I first met Dr. Demming in 1987. He lectured for hours to an enthralled group of manufacturing businessmen. His methods were simple: no flashy video presentations, no slides, no fancy handouts. It was just Dr. Demming, an overhead projector, a blank transparency and a black marker. He began at 8:30 a.m. and by 4 p.m. the audience was exhausted. He noticed the group beginning to doze and admonished us to bear with him for about another hour because he wanted to make a few more important points.

We were all dumbfounded. How could this 90-year-old man keep going? Suddenly, one "40 something" executive jumped up and shouted a question. Dr. Demming's answer was short and simple. The questioner countered with an opposing view. Dr. Demming responded with the same simple answer. The questioner became angry and shouted, "Dr. Demming, why don't you give me a better answer?" Dr. Demming replied, "The answer does not matter, it is the question that is important."

The lecture went on until 6 o'clock, and he announced that some videos about some companies that had implemented his quality-management techniques would be shown at 7:30 p.m. for anyone who was interested.

After dinner, about 7:25 p.m. and with nothing to do, I dropped by the room where the videos were to be shown. There was Dr. Demming sitting in the front row. I sat down beside him and introduced myself. "I certainly learned a lot today," I told him. He smiled that old professor-like smile.

"I didn't expect to see you here," I said. "It's been a long day, and you've seen these videos a hundred times, I'll bet."

"But I might learn something from one of you fellas," he replied.

I learned a lot from Dr. Demming that day. His theories were difficult to implement, but "made in the USA" products are better today because of him.

Some say that as we age, we enter our second childhood. I hope so, because perhaps then I'll acquire the simplistic perspective of a child. Then, I'll regain the child-like inquisitiveness and awe of life.   Then, rather than espousing wisdom, I'll join in the learning. Maybe, I'll even make it to 90.

Thanks Dr. Demming.

❤

Why?

Last week I had the privilege of spending some one-on-one time with my 3-year-old grandson Jake. We were traveling from his house to mine. I was driving my trusty old Honda, and he was safely strapped in his car seat behind me. He could easily see out the windows, and I began the following dialogue:

"Look at those pretty flowers."

"Where?" he asked.

"Over there," I said, pointing to a huge flower bed in a park, "They're so pretty."

"Why?"

"Because God made them that way."

"Why?"

"Because God loves us."

"Why?"

Now, I was getting in way over my head. I thought for a minute, then opted for a comment I hoped would get me out of the complexity he had so deftly steered me into. "I don't know," I said. There was silence, and I breathed a sigh of relief.

"What's God?" came the voice from the back seat. Oh no! This little human being had me trapped again. I took a few more minutes to ponder my answer. Finally I said, "God is a big guy that lives up in heaven, up in the sky, and he takes care of us." I surmised that this simple explanation would be the easiest concept for him to grasp.

"Why?"

"Because God loves us."

"Why?"

"I don't know why!"

Silence.

This scenario continued for an hour or more. I'd make a comment and he"d respond with "why?" or "how?" I was completely exhausted by his relentless inquiries. My throat was sore, my voice was raspy, and my mind was numb.

I've thought about this episode for some time now. I've concluded that in my effort to have a real bonding experience with my grandson, I assumed that I should start by talking. Maybe he would glean some wisdom from his grandpa. Maybe he would learn a little something about the world. Well, I think I was wrong. I think he wanted me to shut up, but was not old enough to tell me so. For Jake, just being together was plenty enough. I didn't have to force a conversation. I had given him a drink from a fire hose when he wasn't even thirsty. All he wanted to do was experience the moment with me, and I had screwed it up by talking.

I've noticed that this "why" period lasts about 6 months before little kids learn that to talk is to "control." They then barrage you with a constant volley of "Papa, you-know-whats" trying to get your attention.

Pretty fast learners, aren't they!

The next time I'm going to try to be quiet and let him lead the conversation. Maybe if I ask "why," I'll learn something.

Thanks Jake.

♥

Raton Road

Dear Zach,

It's Wednesday evening, and I'm flying to Phoenix to see my friend Sam. I'm passing over the mountains that fill the Colorado-New Mexico border. Down there somewhere is a dirt road that goes from Raton, NM, due west for 40 miles to a huge coal mine. At least it was there 25 years ago when I drove it once a month to sell mine roof bolts. It's the most spectacular 40 miles of road I have ever driven.

I'd start out before dawn while the clay on the road was still frozen. If I left later, the road would thaw and on my return trip, the odds of sliding into the ditch or off into a canyon were mighty high.

As I drove west, the sun would rise behind me, touching the snow-capped peaks of the Sangre de Cristos in the distance, coloring them first pale blue, then pink, then a brilliant white. Silhouetted against the deep blue sky, they would literally, take my breath away. Elk, mule deer, and wild turkeys would stir from their snoozings and wander across my path. I tried counting the mule deer one time, but stopped at 100. They were everywhere. I would roll down the windows and breathe in the crisp mountain air. Shivering, I could hardly keep the car on the road trying to see, to smell, to feel and to absorb it all somehow. I'd pinch myself to make sure I wasn't dreaming. It was supernatural. Yes, that's it, "super natur-al."

I don't know why I feel compelled to write to you about all this, other than to share a rekindled feeling that is so precious to me. Maybe it's because I felt God's presence so strongly when I made that trip each month and want to share it with you.

You are a unique child of God. I don't know where your uniqueness will take you, but wherever it does, it's important to be on the lookout for God's presence. He's everywhere, you know.

So find your Raton road. Find lots of them. Travel them regularly, and if you're ever in Northern New Mexico, try one of mine.

Remember to leave before dawn when the road's still frozen. I'm certain God will still be there.

Love,
Papa Gil

❤

Spontaneous

A constant babble was coming from the rear seat of the car as 20-month-old Parker expounded on some subject. I couldn't understand a word he said, but the look on his face through the rear-view mirror spoke of happy anticipation and outright glee as we made the 10-minute drive to the park.

I love to take little ones to the park. It's a great place to talk and to let them learn, plus it's a great place for me to be a kid again.

We bounced out of the car, and Parker took off for the playground. Playgrounds aren't my favorite spots to "play" because one little slip on a rung or one little tumble and we're on our way to the emergency room. Besides, my plan was to hike on the nature trail.

Parker climbed up on a fire truck built out of wood with a metal steering wheel. Immediately, he grabbed it, turning it furiously and making that roaring sound that little boys make when driving trucks on some imaginary mission.

Tired of driving, he leaped from the truck and ran to the swings. His pint-size body stood on tip toe to reach the seat, but he couldn't quite make it. I picked him up and held him on my lap. We swung back and forth making a "wheeee" sound as I pumped the swing higher.

Swinging didn't last long either, and he wailed to stop when he spotted the sliding board. This was no ordinary playground sliding board, but one of those giant metal ones that seemingly reach to the sky. Its shiny metal glistened in the afternoon sun. As the swing came to a halt, I lowered him to the ground. His feet were moving before he hit the dirt, and he bolted toward the sliding board's ladder. Apprehensive of his safety, I climbed the 18 metal rungs close behind him making certain I could catch him if he slipped. We arrived at the top and he looked at me with grinning apprehension. He then turned around and hurled himself down the slide. Grandma, who had come with us, screamed and deftly grabbed him as he exited the silver chute. He was giddy with glee. Grandma and I were clutching our chests with fear! He ran around to the steps to try it again. He was full of joy: no fear, no foresight for trouble, simply enjoying the moment with wild abandon. He spent the next half hour's worth of "moments" going down and up, up and down, down and up.

Finally it was time to go, and we had to bribe him into leaving by promising him an ice cream cone on the way home (it's OK for grandparents to bribe).

I was somewhat disappointed. I had wanted to take him on the nature trail at the far end of the park, but his single-mindedness wrecked my plans. Ahhh, there's the problem. I had "plans", he had "spontaneity". I was planning on communing with nature. Parker had spontaneously communed with a fire truck, briefly with a swing, and intensely with a sliding board instead.

Parker and I will have many trips to the playground. We will have lots of walks in the woods, and on nature trails. I'll spend hours "planning" future adventures. Parker, on the other hand, will save all that planning energy and spend it on enjoying the moment.

Planning is an adult activity. Little ones simply act.

Thanks Parker.

❤

A Gift

It was one of those perfect Indian summer days when the warm sun melts into your skin and the blue sky is indescribably blue. The moving van doors had opened, revealing the accumulation of 38 years of marriage. Two of our grandsons were running around exploring our new place, asking "where can I sleep when I come visit, papa?" and "where will you keep our special toys?" I was concerned about the effect moving would have on these little people. Granted, I probably was overly sensitive to the issue, but that's how grandfathers are.

My job was hooking up the washer and dryer and making sure that all my "stuff" was being properly placed in the garage or the room that was to be my office. Moving men, friends and neighbors were everywhere, scurrying about trying to help get us settled. Finally, I took a break, grabbed a cup of coffee from the pot that was perking away on top of a box of dishes, and sauntered out on the back deck. I eased into the old metal backyard chair I had purchased from the L. L. Bean catalog 20 years ago, and took a sip from the cup. I gazed at the scenery before me and suddenly, noticed I was not alone.

Two-year-old Kari, our only grand-daughter after 5 boys, was standing in the far corner, by the pine tree, staring out into space. She appeared frightened by all the goings on, although I couldn't see her face. Her back was to me. Her curly blond hair was ruffled, and she stood with her arms wrapped around her chest, her little hands peeking at me from around her shoulders. "This is serious stuff," I said to myself. I paused a moment, then cleared my throat, hoping to break her apparent trance. No reaction. I tried it again, but still she did not move. I put down my coffee and walked slowly to her side. Squatting down and putting my hand on her shoulder, I whispered, "Kari, are you feeling sad?" Turning around slowly with her arms still across her chest, she smiled and said in her 2 - year - old way, "no papa, I just give me a hug!"

I don't know if I'll ever really get the hang of this grandfather business: When to speak up. When to keep my mouth shut. When to get involved. When to simply observe. I probably interrupted her free-spirited mind's journey by being too concerned that day, but I did learn a valuable lesson:

A hug is a great gift to give yourself, especially when things seem to be whirling around you.

Thanks Kari.

❤

Peace

I grew up in a big Lutheran church in a small town in western Pennsylvania. It was a huge, red brick monolith with a tall bell tower. When the bells rang they could be heard all over town. Our pastor, Gordon Huffman, was dearly loved by the entire congregation. All the kids were involved in youth groups, choirs and Sunday School and the church was packed every Sunday. However, Dr. Huffman was unbending in his adherence to Lutheran doctrine, and attending confirmation class was like sitting at the foot of a Lutheran oak.

Apparently, I was more interested in the social aspects of youth groups because, although I was taught everything, I learned very little. For instance, the meaning of the word 'peace' never sunk in. I thought it was the opposite of war. Ashamedly, only in the past 10 years or so, have I come to really understand the 'peace of God.'

Maybe it's like a lot of things we are

taught. We memorize things like The Lord's Prayer, the National Anthem and the Pledge of Allegiance without really thinking about the meaning.

Awhile back, our eighth grandchild, Dylan Christopher Schorr, was born. One evening, I watched as he snoozed in his mother's arms. So comfortable. So unconcerned for his safety. No worries. No concern about the future. No rehashing the past. Wanting nothing. Just 'being.' So peaceful.

Dylan is 9 months old now, and is still full of peace. His brothers rough him up now and then, and his parents don't pay as much attention to his occasional whimper as they used to, but all in all, Dylan has peace.

I believe we are born with perfect peace and then spend most of our lives scurrying around losing it. When we finally discover that we don't have it anymore, we scurry around searching for it, yearning for it, desperate for it. If we are lucky, we come to realize that 'peace' didn't go anywhere, it's been within us from the day we were born. It is a gift of God.

Oh, I'm pretty certain Dylan will spend some time losing it. Then he'll spend some time searching for it. Hopefully, he'll discover it again—and it won't take him as long as it took me. You see, it's not a matter of finding, it's a matter of letting go. Just like the miners of yesteryear, who searched these Colorado mountains for gold, we must get rid of a lot of the stuff on top, to find the treasure buried underneath.

Thanks Dylan.

God's Peace to you.

❤